THE VET'S ASSISTANT

Inspirational Amish Romance

HANNAH MILLER

Tica House
Publishing

Sweet Romance that Delights and Enchants!

Personal Word from the Author

To My Dear Readers,

How exciting that you have chosen one of my books to read. Thank you! I am proud to now be part of the team of writers at Tica House Publishing who work joyfully to bring you stories of hope, faith, courage, and love.

Please feel free to contact me as I love to hear from my readers. I would like to personally invite you to sign up for updates and to become part of our **Exclusive Reader Club** —it's completely Free to join! Hope to see you there!

With love,

Hannah Miller

VISIT HERE to Join our Reader's Club and to Receive Tica House Updates:

http://ticahousepublishing.subscribemenow.com

Chapter One

March 4th

I love my job. And I love my family, I do. Sometimes though... sometimes I feel like I'm torn, like I have to choose one or the other, and either way, I'm going to end up unhappy.

What is happiness, anyway? And is Gott *concerned that we be happy?*

I'm in love with an Englischer. *It's impossible. I am at odds with myself. My heart is rebelling against me—and against* Gott. *I can never be with the* Englischer. *I know that. I have been baptized, and he never will be.*

But oh, he's a good man. He's not one of our people, but he's a good Christian, and he cares, more than anyone else I've ever met, for Gott's *creatures.*

I know I'm lucky to have my job, to be allowed outside of the community as I am. My family, my district, trust me. I'm afraid that trust is misplaced. Why should they trust me when I cannot trust myself?

I'm so torn, Diary.

Yours, Rachel.

Rachel crouched, the filing cabinet drawer open in front of her. Her predecessor had, for some unknown reason, filed everything under first name instead of surname. Although Rachel had re-organized everything her first week on the job, sometimes things still turned up out of place.

"What are you muttering about?"

Mason's voice made her jump.

She stood, straightening her apron. "Just filing stuff," she said, smiling. "I'll fix it."

Mason smiled back, and Rachel's heart fluttered. "I know you will," he said. "You always do." He laid a hand on her shoulder, and the fluttering became a full electric zap. "You're the best receptionist I've ever had."

Rachel laughed at that, although it came out shrill and nervous. "I doubt that," she said.

"No. I'll admit I had my reservations, but you're very

efficient. And you're great with the animals. Speaking of which... While Katrina's away sunning herself in Mexico, I thought perhaps you'd like to assist me with consultations."

Rachel's mouth opened and then closed again. Mason wanted *her* to assist him? True, she knew about animals—although her family was mainly in the furniture business, they farmed too, and she'd been around animals her whole life. Still, she was no vet, nor even a vet nurse. She didn't have the training... And yet he wanted *her*. Not Cara, who was actually qualified and right now was just out the back cleaning down the pens. No, he'd asked *her*.

"Is... that a yes?"

Rachel nodded, still finding it hard to speak. What was this strange mix of feelings whirling through her? Pride, with a flicker of anxiety and a pinch of excitement. She would have to be careful of that. There was a good reason for pride being included in the worst of sins.

"Great. Because I've got an appointment at ten o' clock, out at that sanctuary place. You know the one?"

Rachel knew the one. The sanctuary was infamous among the local farmers, although Rachel had found the women who owned it to be very pleasant. She'd certainly be interested to see what it was really like out there.

And she was going with Mason. The thought had her humming to herself as she turned back to the filing cabinet.

Mason took a waiting patient, a young border collie with a limp, through to consultation room A.

The road turned off onto a dirt path. Rachel hadn't ridden in many cars, but it wasn't entirely new to her. Her family often hired a Mennonite driver to take them places too far for their buggy. What *was* new was sitting this close to Mason, his hand occasionally brushing her knee as he shifted gears in the old manual. She wanted to touch his hand, to press his fingers to her cheek. *Healing hands*, she thought. What might they heal in her?

Ashamed of such thoughts, she took in a deep breath and ignored his cursory glance. He brought the vehicle to a stop before a metal gate, and she seized the chance to jump out the door and open it. Her hands were trembling.

She stood back as Mason drove through the gate. The van stopped. He was waiting for her. She closed the gate and got back in the van. It smelled of straw, faintly animal-y, and closer, of Mason. He wore no aftershave, but the scent of disinfectant still clung to his skin. His gaze met hers, his dark eyes watchful. There was something in them... something that made her want to lean in and...

Rachel turned her gaze to the window. She could still feel his eyes on her, but she ignored it as best she could. Mason started the engine again, and they crawled forward, up the drive, mindful of the roosters darting about. When she opened the door again, the air was full of crowing. Nearby, but out of sight, a sheep bleated, and a cow lowed. From inside the house, dogs were barking.

A woman emerged from the front door, her hair buzzed short. She was followed by another woman, with longer, greying blond hair. The first woman strode toward them. She wore rain boots with denim shorts and a dirty white tank top. She held out a hand to Rachel, dirt under her fingernails, and smiled warmly as Rachel shook it.

"I'm Donna," she introduced herself. "This is Mary." She gestured behind herself to the other, taller, woman. "Where's Katrina?"

Mason smiled. "Lounging on a beach in Mexico, I expect. Rachel's assisting me today."

Donna nodded, then turned abruptly on her heel, striding up the path. Roosters and geese reluctantly shifted themselves out of their way as Mason and Rachel followed her.

The patient was corralled in a small pen that narrowed to a point. It was Jemma, Rachel remembered from the file, a saddleback pig about six years old. Jemma ran toward an apple as Donna threw it, no sign of the limp they were here to check. Once the apple was gone, however, Jemma raised her left back leg, teetering.

"Hi there," Rachel crooned as she slipped through the gate behind Donna.

Jemma squealed, turning and rushing over to the corner, putting as much distance between herself and them as she could.

Mason said, "How long has she had the limp?"

"About a week," Mary told him. "It was subtle at first, but it's gotten worse very quickly."

"Okay," Mason said. "We need to get her in the crush and sedate her." He turned to Rachel. "Rachel, can you get me the snare loop?"

Rachel turned and let herself out of the pen, heading quickly for the back of the van. She found the snare easily and brought it to Mason, who took it with a murmured thanks before focusing again on his patient.

This was one of the things Rachel most admired about her boss. He was, at all times, professional and matter-of-fact. He was a quiet man, studious, with thoughts that ran deep, and an ability to really listen that was rare in the men Rachel had known in her life.

She snapped her attention back to the matter at hand and watched from the other side as Donna lured Jemma into the narrow end of the pen—the crush, albeit a makeshift one— by throwing bread and apples. Once Jemma was in there, Mason slipped the noose of the snare quickly over Jemma's head and tightened it. At the same time, Donna pushed Jemma forward with a wood pallet from behind, trapping her in.

Jemma screamed. It was high-pitched, frenzied, as she tried to escape but couldn't. It had been a while since Rachel had heard a pig scream like that. The sound cut right through her, and she forced herself to remain calm.

Rachel barely noticed Mason sticking Jemma with the needle, so focused was she on Jemma's face, her panicked mouth opening and closing as she tried to wriggle free.

Soon, Jemma fell quiet and slipped onto her knees, the sedative taking effect.

Mason got to work.

Jemma's hoof had overgrown, ulcered and burst, leaving a crack in the trotter that was festering. Rachel fetched things from the van as ordered, and watched Mason open up and clean out the wound. When it was done, he stood up, brushed off his sea-green overalls, and pursed his lips.

"We're probably going to need to do this again," he told Donna and Mary. "Unfortunately, I don't think she's going to help us with keeping it clean. I'd say about a week from now, to check how it's going and clean it again, and then we'll see from there."

He talked them through the aftereffects of the sedative, and Rachel listened quietly as Mary questioned him about another matter—a duck with an ear infection. They clearly cared about their animals.

"Thanks, Mason," Donna said, shooting him a warm smile, like they were old friends. "I'll see you both out."

They turned to walk down the path, Mason in front with Donna, discussing Jemma's care, while Rachel trailed behind.

She didn't see the rooster coming up behind her until it was too late. Sharp claws scraped through her thick black stockings, tearing flesh. She screamed, whirling around. The rooster was a dark red, the feathers around his neck frilled up. He came at her again, side on. This time, she was able to get her foot up, and he threw himself into the sole of her shoe, rebounding.

"Julian!" Donna shouted, marching up to the rooster. He backed off but shot Rachel a beady-eyed scowl.

"Are you all right?" Mason asked, his tone concerned.

Rachel lifted her chin and nodded. Her calf hurt where the rooster had caught her, likely bruised her, too, but it wasn't as though she hadn't been bitten or scratched before. She'd live.

"Are you sure you're all right?" Mason asked again, this time as they drove down the long, winding road back to town.

"Yes, I'm sure," she told him. "I'm not made of glass."

Mason chuckled. "No," he said. "There's steel in you. Still, I want to take a look when we're back at the surgery. If he's broken the skin, the wound will need cleaning."

Rachel couldn't fault his pragmatism, but the wound was almost knee height—there was no way she was going to let him look at it. Why, she'd have to raise her skirt. Besides, it would be fine once cleaned up with some hot water and a home solution, and she could do that very well by herself.

Back at the surgery, Rachel had almost forgotten about the wound. They had appointments starting again in half an hour, and she needed to go through the phone messages, and, she supposed, grab a quick lunch.

But almost as soon as she had sat down in the office chair, Mason leaned over the desk. "Did you think you were getting away with it?" he said, a teasing smile playing at his lips.

It was easy to become distracted by those lips. She wondered what they would feel like against her cheek. She wanted to touch his face, to feel his sun-freckled skin and three-day stubble. Instead, she straightened, her shoulders stiffening.

"Come on," he said. "Show me."

"It's fine," Rachel assured him, her tone sterner than she'd meant it to be. "Nothing but a scratch, I promise you."

He held up his hands, surprise flitting across his face. "All right," he said. "But don't blame me when you come down with tetanus."

Rachel rolled her eyes at him, but something warm glowed in her chest. Mason *cared*. He cared about *her*. She could see that in his eyes, impossibly green under the bright strip lights, focused on her.

"Your next appointment's due in ten minutes," she said, just as sternly.

He stood, cleared his throat, nodded and thanked her. Then he turned and walked briskly off into the consulting room.

Rachel was torn between congratulating herself on avoiding temptation and kicking herself for being so rude. She had to keep Mason at arm's length, yes, but there was no need to be unkind. That wasn't the sort of person she wanted to be. No, she would have to make more of an effort.

Chapter Two

Rachel spent that afternoon organizing files and cleaning up messes made by the clients. It was quieter than usual though, with only one old cat staying in for observation after a surgery early that morning. By four in the afternoon, even he had vacated.

Rachel was preparing to leave when Mason approached her. "Thanks for today," he said.

She shook her head. "I can't say I did much," she told him.

"No, but it's good to have backup, and you were very efficient, did everything you were asked to do when you were asked. Believe it or not, not everyone is capable of that."

Rachel's cheeks warmed, and she bid him goodnight. He cast her one last look before he locked the door behind them. She headed for the rack where she'd put her bike. Quickly rearranging her skirts, she pedaled off into the bright spring evening.

She swung into the small farmstead where her family lived and parked the bike around the back by the storage shed. Hens clucked around her feet, not yet away for the night, and, judging by their behaviour, not yet fed. Before heading inside, she went into the feed shed and scooped a seed mix into a bowl, scattering it on the ground outside and scattering even more of it into the large coop that would house them all for the night.

She then headed inside.

"How was work?" William asked as she walked in the door.

Rachel didn't miss *Dat's* sharp look, but William must have. She knew her father disapproved of her job, of its supposed '*Englisch* influence.' Still, he didn't mind accepting the pay from it, so he kept quiet and let it be. Rachel was glad of that, at least. She didn't quite know what she would do without her job, without being able to see Mason every day.

"Well?" William said, when Rachel's pause had grown a little too long. "Or are you working as a government spy now and have been sworn to secrecy?"

William was two years older than she was, and, like both

Rachel and Adam— who was between them in age—still unmarried. While the three of them still lived at home, her brother Job had moved onto his own property, a twenty-acre farm a few miles down the road.

"It was amazing," Rachel admitted, once *Dat* had turned away again, a clear indication that he was no longer listening to their conversation. "Katrina—she's the vet nurse—is away for a few weeks so I'm helping Mason with his rounds. He told me I'm the best receptionist he's ever had."

Adam raised an eyebrow. "You want to watch that, Rachel. You know what *Englischers* can be like."

Rachel frowned. Mason wasn't like that. Not at all. If only they knew him. But no, they never would. Of course, they had met him, had talked business, but that wasn't the same thing at all.

She was distracted from a reply by her mother calling from the kitchen. "Rachel dear, come and help me for a moment."

Secretly, Rachel thought she must have overheard the conversation, and known the direction it was going, and that they would all end up silently angry with each other and dinner would be eaten in tense frustration. She turned her back on her brothers and walked into the kitchen with her head held high.

"Hello, *Mamm*," she said, and kissed her mother on the cheek before sitting down to help peel potatoes.

"I forgot to say this morning," *Mamm* told her, "But we have a guest coming to dinner."

A guest? It had been a while since they'd had guests for dinner mid-week.

"Yes. A few, actually. Your brother is coming, and Lloyd Werngard, too. You remember Lloyd? It's been so long since any of us have seen him outside of work, and you know he's all alone on that farm of his now that his father has passed and his sisters have both married."

Rachel nodded. As if she could forget Lloyd. Dear Lloyd, with his long nose and pale eyes, and his bad jokes. She saw him often at church, but it had been almost a year since she'd last spoken to him properly. When was that, exactly? Perhaps a month or two after his father had died.

Lloyd had retreated a little, grown quiet, and often didn't answer the door when Adam or William went over to check on him. He'd opened the door for Rachel, though, although he hadn't said much, only thanked her for the stew she and *Mamm* had made and bid her a good day.

It was Martha she'd been friends with, really, his youngest sister, but he'd always been around. Of course, she hadn't spoken to Martha in a while either, not outside of church. She was busy, Rachel supposed, being a new mother and all, and Rachel had been busy too, with her job and with the book-keeping for her family's furniture business.

"That will be nice," she said. Aside from Lloyd, it was always nice to see her brother, Job and his wife, Catherine.

They worked in silence for a while, Rachel chopping vegetables while her mother prepared the meat.

Supper was almost ready when a knock on the door announced the first of their guests' arrival. It was Lloyd, exactly on time as usual. He was shortly followed by Job and Catherine. Rachel waved to them from across the front room, receiving a smile from Catherine and a nod from Job. Rachel then retreated to the relative quiet of the kitchen, where her mother stood by the stove, poking a fork into the potatoes to see if they were ready.

Catherine hovered in the doorway for a moment, as if not quite sure of herself, until *Mamm* asked her to lay dishes around the long table in the dining room. She quickly obeyed, grateful for something to do.

"How's the new barn coming along?" Rachel asked her.

"The barn?" Catherine asked, blinking twice, then, "Oh, *jah*. Well, it's built, just needs a touch of paint now. We'll have other things to think about soon, though."

"Oh?" Rachel asked, setting down the last of the plates while Catherine laid cutlery.

Catherine smoothed down her apron and cleared her throat. "Well..."

"Watch out, girls, coming through," *Mamm* said, angling past Rachel with a ceramic pot that was steaming from under the lid. "Rachel, please tell the others that supper is ready."

Soon they were all gathered around while *Mamm* set the last of the dishes on the table.

They lowered their heads, clasping hands, while *Dat* led them in silent prayer. Rachel eyed the dishes on the table, as their rich, warm scents filled the room, and wondered at *Gott's* bounty. They were truly blessed to have such riches, to be able to eat until they were full, and such delicious foods too, straight from the earth.

"So, Lloyd," *Dat* said, when everyone had filled their plates. "How's the farm?"

"It's doing all right," Lloyd answered slowly. "As you know, I've scaled things back a little, but we'll be planting the wheat soon, and some new saplings in the orchard."

Dat nodded. "Sensible," he decided. "Now there's not so many of you to work the fields. Have you thought about selling off?"

Lloyd shook his head. "Not as yet. I'll see how the next year or so goes before I make any big decisions."

"I must say it's right nice to see you again, Lloyd," *Mamm* said. "We were so sorry about your father's death."

Lloyd thanked her and fell quiet, his gaze cast down to his dinner plate.

Rachel felt a surge of sympathy for him. He clearly still felt his father's loss—and why wouldn't he? Rachel couldn't imagine losing either of her parents. Luckily, they were still relatively young and quite fit and healthy. Still, one could never tell...

"Well if you need any help with the planting—or the harvest later down the road, you let us know," *Dat* said. "William and Adam will be only too happy to help out, won't you, boys?"

Both boys nodded as they chewed.

"I thank you," Lloyd said. "But I should be all right."

"What about you, Job?" Adam asked suddenly. "Anything interesting happening out your way? I saw the new barn when I was walking past the other day. Looks *gut*."

Job cleared his throat. "Actually, there is something interesting." He looked to Catherine, who nodded in answer to some silent question. "Catherine's in the family way."

Mamm gasped, and *Dat* stood, coming around the table to clap Job on the shoulder. This was what Catherine had wanted to tell her earlier, Rachel realized, when they were setting the table. She was going to be an *aenti*! She found herself unable to control the smile creeping onto her face. "Congratulations," she said, and made a mental note to keep her brother and her sister-in-law in her prayers that night and every night until the little one was born.

"You're going to be an *aenti*," Lloyd said, after dinner, when everyone was on their way out. "How does it feel?"

"*Gut*," Rachel told him. "Although, I'll have to brush up on my knitting skills."

Lloyd smiled at that. "Well, at least *boppli* clothes are small," he said. "Talking of *bopplis*," he said, to Adam and William now as well as Rachel, "Bess has had her first litter. Perhaps you'd all like to come and see the puppies some time?"

His gaze flickered to Rachel, who quickly glanced away. She felt awkward, as though there was some other motive in Lloyd's asking. She knew, really, why he'd been asked here, why her parents kept extending invitations to him. They hoped she and Lloyd would get together. But Rachel only had eyes for one man, and it wasn't Lloyd.

"You should have asked while Job was still here," Adam said. "His old dog, Horace passed last month. He might like a young pup."

"Not with the *boppli* due, surely?" Rachel said. "Puppies are such a pain to train."

Lloyd chuckled. "A pain to train... Nice rhyming skills there, Rachel."

Rachel rolled her eyes at him, and his smile turned sheepish.

Still, she thought, coming back to the idea of a young dog for Job, a new puppy, and a new baby... The two would go well together, wouldn't they? Or perhaps that was fanciful thinking. *Dat* had always said she was full of fancy. Rachel supposed he was right. She had always lived half in a dream world, and still did now. She thought about giving one of the young collies to Mason. His birthday would be coming up in a few months. But no, he wouldn't like that. He hated the idea of giving animals as gifts. Still...

She shook her head, telling herself not to be so ridiculous, and bid Lloyd a good night as he headed out.

Chapter Three

Dear Diary,

I know Mamm *and* Dat *are eager for me to like Lloyd as more than just a friend. I feel like dinner last night was just a set up. But how can I love Lloyd when I already love Mason? Can a person love two men at once? I don't believe I can.*

Lloyd is a good man, and his family and mine have been friends since before either of us were born. It's true we haven't seen much of them since old Josiah Werngard passed away, but that connection is still there... Really, it would be a great solution. For my parents, and for me. Perhaps not for Lloyd—he deserves a woman who can love him fully with her whole heart.

It would be simpler, perhaps, to give up on Mason and to start something new with Lloyd, but oh... I just don't know how to feel about him. Yes, I like him, but it's not love. Not LOVE, in all capitals like that.

I know what my mother would say. She would tell me that love isn't everything, and do I think she loved my father when she married him? She's said as much before, and it makes me feel rather sorry for Dat. But she loves him now, I suppose. I can see that well enough.

I feel lost, Diary. Like my life is spinning out in all directions, and I don't know which thread to choose.

I must pray for guidance.

Yours,

Rachel.

Rachel woke the next morning before the sun had risen. The sky was a dark mauve, heralding the oncoming dawn. Before getting out of bed, she picked out her diary from under the mattress and wrote a short entry. Scanning back through the pages, Mason's name stood out several times. *Mason.* Honestly, she ought to put him out of her mind. Almost six months she'd worked at his practice. She should be able to get over this silly feeling about him. It wasn't at all practical.

She quickly washed and dressed and went out to free the hens and scatter some seed for them. She fed the goats and then returned inside to help her mother prepare breakfast. William led in silent prayer, and they ate together, mostly in quiet—the men in Rachel's family were not true morning people, although routine dictated they at least behave otherwise. Rachel loved eating meals all together with her family, even when they weren't saying much. It was a pleasant feeling, knowing she was surrounded by people who cared about her. Sharing a meal was, *Mamm* had always said, showing love for one another.

When she went back outside to collect the family bicycle, however, her day took a downturn. The front wheel was punctured. When it had happened, Rachel couldn't imagine— she hadn't noticed anything wrong on her ride home the day before. It was simple enough to fix but doing so would make her late, and she didn't want to be late.

"What are you frowning at?" Adam asked her as he entered the shed.

Rachel quickly wiped the scowl from her face and gestured at the bicycle.

Adam chuckled. "Perhaps *Gott* has answered our prayers—you won't be able to work for those *Englischers* anymore, eh?"

Rachel's scowl returned. She knew he was teasing, but there was some truth in his words. Her family had never been especially pleased about her job, although they were only too happy to accept the money it gave her.

"Come on Rachel, cheer up. Look, it's easily mended."

"But I'll be late!"

"If you are, then it's *Gott's* will. You can't fight that."

Rachel sighed. She supposed he was right. She would get to work when she got there. She just hoped Mason wouldn't worry about her absence. She had no way to let him know she'd be late. If only she had a phone.

She shook her head. That was *Englisch* thinking. Maybe her family was right/ In a way, the *Englisch* were having some influence on her. She checked herself, taking a deep breath. Things would work out. They always did.

"Or you could ask William to give you a lift," Adam said then. "He said he was heading that way today."

Rachel's world brightened, just a little, and she turned and hurried back up to the house, where William was already putting on his coat and straw hat. She straightened her *kapp* and told him the problem. "If you're going that way, would you mind taking me? And possibly picking me up later?"

"Of course," he said, and Rachel's heart lifted a little. "I know you too well. You'd be trying to walk there and back if I didn't take you."

"Don't be silly. I'd fix the bicycle before that."

"You'd better do that tonight anyway. I won't be going this way tomorrow, so if your tire's still flat you really will be walking."

He helped Rachel up onto the cart and then hoisted himself

up beside her. The pony cart was old and well-used, but it still had many years left in it. Rachel preferred the buggy, though, as she felt safer on the road with it. But the pony cart was easier to hitch up and easier to drive.

Adam dropped her off just down the road from the practice, and she walked from there.

"I was starting to worry," Mason said, glancing at the clock on the wall behind them, and then back at her. She was half an hour early, but still twenty minutes later than her usual time. "Thought I'd have to call out a search party."

She smiled and told him the story, and he nodded, understanding. He always understood. That was one of the things she liked so much about him.

"Oh well. It's given me a chance to have a second cup of coffee before you start talking my ear off."

Rachel mock-scowled at him. "As if I would," she said. "I'll have you. My *mammi* says I'm too quiet."

Mason chuckled. "Well I'm sure your grandmother's right. Elderly people are always all knowing. Or at least *my* grandmother certainly seems to be."

It was Rachel's turn to laugh, then, as she turned her back to Mason to check the phone for messages. She made several notes to call people back and deleted any irrelevant calls.

"Tea?" Mason asked. "It sounds like you've had a hectic morning."

"Thank you," Rachel said. "But I've made my morning sound much worse than it was, really. A flat tire isn't much more than a minor inconvenience."

Mason nodded. "Yes, I did figure you for a drama queen."

A drama queen? Rachel was sure what he meant, but he retreated into the staffroom to prepare the tea.

It never tasted quite the same as it did at home—all quick, with teabags and an electric kettle—but still, a warm drink early in the morning, especially after a stressful start, was just what she needed to relax and focus on the day ahead.

Rachel was mopping down the reception area for the last time that evening when the door opened. She'd been expecting to meet William at the point where he'd dropped her off. The road Mason's veterinary practice was on was potholed and rutted—not entirely suitable for the family's cart, or for the horses' feet. When she looked up from the spot she'd been mopping, though, she saw not William, but Lloyd.

"Oh," she said, surprise raising her eyebrows slightly. "Are you my lift home, then?"

Lloyd smiled and gave her a slight bow. "If it suits," he said.

"Well, of course." She paused. "But why isn't William picking me up?"

"I'm not sure. Your *mamm* just said he was busy, and since I was going that way, perhaps I could help out. And of course, I was only too happy to."

"Well," she said, smiling. "Thank you. Take a seat and I'll be finished here in about five minutes." Of course, she knew exactly what her mother was up to. She would have thought she was being subtle, of course, but Rachel knew her too well. Poor Lloyd. She doubted William was busy at all, or else he'd been sent off on some unnecessary errand meant to waylay him.

Rachel spent the next five minutes throwing out the water from the mop bucket, straightening items on the desk, and bidding Mason goodnight. Mason smiled warmly at her.

"See you tomorrow," he promised, and Rachel smiled in return. Yes, she would see him tomorrow. The thought made her heart flutter. How lucky she was, to be able to spend time with Mason, even if only through work. She was truly blessed.

Rachel followed Lloyd out to where he'd left the cart and climbed up into it. The evening was cool, and she wrapped her cloak tighter around her shoulders.

"How was work?" Lloyd asked.

"It's been a long day," she admitted. "We had an emergency with a dog that had been hit by a car. Honestly, Lloyd, I could have cried. Her owner couldn't even get her out of the car because her insides were hanging out."

Lloyd's lips thinned and Rachel almost regretted telling the story. It was rather grim, she supposed. Certainly not something to tell over supper, at least. But Lloyd was robust, had to be as a farmer.

"Mason was so good though," she said, hoping to cheer things up a bit. "He went out there, and we wrapped the poor thing up in a sheet and brought her in. Mason was in surgery for hours with that dog, and do you know? She's pulled through. She'll have to stay in for a few nights, of course, to be sure, but... We're hopeful."

Another thought occurred to her. "Mason's even taking her home with him, so she won't be alone overnight. Honestly, Lloyd, you'd like him. He really is wonderful. So thoughtful and good with the animals." She couldn't help the smile that crept across her face at the thought of him.

A glance at Lloyd's face, though, told her that Lloyd didn't agree. His mouth was still set in that grim, thin line, an unhappy look in his eyes. Perhaps he was like the rest of her family and disapproved of her working for an *Englischer*. But what business was that of his, when the bishop and her parents had approved it?

They travelled in silence for a little while, until Rachel had to break the tension around them. "How are Bess and her new pups?"

"Right well," Lloyd said. "They're putting on weight nicely, eyes open. And Bess seems very happy. It's funny really, how pleased she looks with herself whenever they're all gathered around her. She has such a human way about her sometimes."

Rachel laughed at that. "I miss having a dog," she admitted. "I don't know if you remember Georgie, our old dog. He was quite disobedient though. I think he put *Dat* off dogs entirely."

Lloyd's expression cracked into a smile. "Sometimes," he said, "I think those are the best kind of dogs. Not exactly what you want, necessarily, but I have to admit I like that sort of wild spirit."

They talked for a while about dogs and about Lloyd's sheep, and Rachel's goats. Rachel had forgotten how pleasant talking to Lloyd could be. She'd always liked him, thought him a decent sort of person, and she couldn't deny that he made her laugh. She knew her mother's hopes for them to court, of course, and still couldn't help but feel that this ride was some connivance of hers.

If only her mother knew how besotted she was over Mason, perhaps she wouldn't have bothered. Or, more likely, perhaps she would try even harder. Rachel couldn't help but feel a little guilty, in a way, that Lloyd's efforts were in vain, but she also knew that he wasn't the sort to hold it against her. Lloyd had never been the type to chase women. Unlike Adam, who had spent most of his *rumspringa* with a different girl every week. Or so Rachel had been told... Rachel knew not to listen too closely to gossip, but knowing her brother as she did, she couldn't help but think it rather likely. Adam wasn't sensible like William and Job. Rachel supposed he was more like her in that sense. Far too fanciful.

Lloyd dropped her off at the end of her drive, not bothering to come up the long driveway to the house. Rachel understood, of course. Her mother would ply him with tea and treats and tell him what a nice young man he was. Lloyd had always been a rather more solitary type, a little nervous, even. He was sweet though, and Rachel almost wished he would come in, just for a while. She couldn't deny she enjoyed his company, albeit just as a good friend.

She waved good-bye to Lloyd and headed up the hill toward home.

Chapter Four

Mud lined the hem of Rachel's skirt; her shoes were caked in it. It had rained that morning and for most of the previous night, and the small-holding they had come out to visit had become almost boggy in places. Mason was covered worse than she was though—his overalls were splattered with brown, and not all of it mud. He had his hand halfway inside a young brown Friesian cow, who was just beginning to bellow again. She had gone quiet for a while, until Mason, Rachel, and the farmer, an elderly man called Kieran Peters, had herded her into a corner of an otherwise almost-empty shed that served as a sort of crush.

Rachel had fetched Mason's bag and watched as Mason manipulated the not-yet-born calf inside its mother's birth canal. It was a breach, Mason had said. Rachel had suspected as much. She'd seen that a few times on her grandparents' farm when she was young. The birthing process wasn't progressing properly, and Mason had found the calf back to front, with its rear hooves facing outward. It was stuck.

Mason shook his head. "I can't get it," he said. "I think we're going to need a calf puller."

Rachel frowned. Mason had as good as told her on the ride over that calf pullers could be dangerous.

"Let me try," she said. What harm could it do? She'd done it before, after all, and she knew what was safe, and when to stop.

Mason glanced at Kieran, who nodded his assent. "Can't see you'll have much luck," Kieran said, "But it's worth a try before we get that contraption on it."

Rachel sterilized her hands at Mason's orders, and pulled on a pair of long, over-the-elbow plastic gloves. Gently, she pushed her hand inside the cow.

Yes, there, she could feel it. As Mason had said, the calf was facing the wrong direction. She grabbed hold of it, gently jostling the calf, manipulating it so that it might—just might —be able to come out. Then she pulled. She remained gentle, but firm, her grip never slipping. And then, the calf's hooves were out. Mason stepped in then, to help her pull the calf out safely.

Kieran tried to comfort the cow, but there wasn't much he

could do there. The beast shook her head from side to side, up and down, eyes rolling. She stamped her hoof.

"Okay," Mason said. "I think we've got it. Yes, there it is. Okay, it's coming."

Rachel stepped aside as Mason tugged gently at the calf, guiding it, and then, he stood back and lowered the calf, a black shape with spindly-looking legs, to the ground. He stood back, then, as Kieran opened up the bars penning her in, so the cow could turn and lick her calf.

It was a wonderful moment. Rachel wanted to clutch Mason's hand as they watched that mother-child bond begin to form. But of course, she didn't. She kept her hands firmly by her sides.

They watched until the calf stood, showing no signs at all of its earlier struggle, and began to suck from its mother.

"Thank you," Kieran said. "I thought I was going to lose the calf for sure, if not the mother."

Mason told him to call them if he had any further problems, and to keep a close eye on both mother and calf for the next few days. Rachel followed Mason out to the car. She brushed down her dress and apron—although both were too much of a mess now for it to do any good—and straightened her *kapp*.

Mason stood for a moment, his hands in the pockets of his overalls, his rain boots swapped again for sneakers more suitable for driving. A light breeze pushed his dark curls slightly to one side. For a moment he looked as though he was about to say something, but then he didn't.

"I hope they'll be all right now," Rachel said. They had seen the calf suckle, but that was no guarantee, especially with one so small.

"Me too," Mason said. "A shame really, that after all that it should be a bull. All that work, and he'll be killed at a few months old."

"Maybe not," Rachel said, trying to lift his spirits. She could see him growing discouraged.

Mason looked at her then, seeming to snap out of his brief melancholy. "Thank you for your help back there," he said. "I couldn't have done it without you. Most likely I couldn't do *anything* without you. You're priceless, Rachel Raber."

Rachel's breath caught. She felt her cheeks go hot. "You know as well as I do that anyone would want to help out in such a situation—and that's why I came, after all."

He shook his head. "No, not everyone would know what to do, or be able to follow instruction so efficiently. You were amazing."

Rachel forced herself to take his comments lightly. "You're going to fill my head with mad ideas about myself if you're not careful," she scolded. Still, she couldn't help the small smile twitching at the corners of her lips.

Mason smiled, too, a broad thing that dimpled his cheeks and lit up his face. "*Sensible* ideas. *True* ideas. Honestly, Rachel, if I didn't love you before today, I certainly do now."

Rachel felt the bottom of the world drop away beneath her feet. Had he really said that, or had she imagined it?

Mason's face went a deep red, then, colour spreading from his cheeks outward. "I mean... uh... I'm sor—"

Without thinking, Rachel reached across to him, and clasped his right hand in both of hers. She held it a moment, savouring the feel of the calloused skin of his palm, the ridges of his knuckles, the dark hairs on the back of his hand. Just as suddenly, she let go, mortified at her actions. She'd gone too far... Surely, God would not be pleased.

Mason was smiling again, his colour now only a slight pink.

"We have to get back," Rachel said quickly and nearly ran around the van to the passenger side.

Mason got into the vehicle on the driver's side, and all the distance Rachel had tried to put between them in that previous moment was gone.

"I think," Mason said slowly, his eyes on the road as he put the van into gear. "We have a lot to discuss."

Rachel took in a deep breath. She felt as though the sun were shining down on her, and she wanted nothing more in that moment than to bask in its warmth; yet on the horizon were thick, dark clouds, a storm approaching.

Dare she believe it? Did Mason feel the same way about her as she did about him? Could something that glorious, that amazing happen to her? But then reality shoved its way into her thoughts and all the reasons against her and Mason, those reasons that had gone around and around in her head since the day she'd realized she loved him, none of them had disappeared.

Still, she could have this one moment, couldn't she?

"Maybe later," she eked out, now feeling completely self-conscious. She couldn't get out of the van soon enough.

Dear Diary,

I know it's not right, but I'm so happy. I think Mason loves me. I love him. Oh, it should be so simple, now we both know. But I feel that things are even more complicated than before. It was safe, I suppose, when I didn't know how he felt. I could pretend nothing would ever happen, while hoping that it would. Now, I don't know what I want. Will I have to make a decision? Will I have to choose one life or the other? And how could Mason win, over Gott, over my church...

Everything I am... is Amish. And Mason... Mason just isn't.

I wish things were different.

I will need to pray for guidance. Isn't that funny? That I need Gott, and church, even more now? No, perhaps it's not funny at all. I can't help but be happy, but I feel that soon... Soon I will be unhappy again.

Yours,

Rachel.

Rachel's heart sang even as her mind whirred, flipping everything over and over again. She wasn't sure if she was happy or afraid. Mason felt the same way she did... But that was a recipe for disaster. Perhaps he could be baptized, but Rachel knew in her heart that would never happen. If they were to be together, she would have to leave home, and that, too, would never happen.

She was no *Englischer*; although she had one foot in their world, she wasn't one of them and wouldn't want to be.

She cycled into work that morning, ignoring the curious stares of early commuters and *Englisch* children on their way to school. She was used to them gawking at her. What she wasn't used to was the internal whirlwind of thoughts and emotions inside of herself. Part of her wanted to believe in happy endings, and the other part knew that she had to make a choice, if not now then soon: Mason or God. There was no contest, of course. But her heart still wanted...

Mason was always at the practice before anyone else—an early riser. There had never been a time when Rachel had gotten there before him, despite her best efforts. Still, she had a key, so when she didn't see his car in the parking lot, she opened the side door and let herself in.

She switched on the lights, her curiosity growing. Where was he? Some early morning emergency call, perhaps? But there was no note on the desk, nothing on the phone's answering machine.

She switched on the computer and logged in. Curiosity grew into worry. She checked his online calendar, and his paper one —nothing.

Eight o' clock came and went. Cara arrived at a quarter past, late as usual, and frowned when Rachel told her Mason wasn't here yet.

"He's always here," she said.

Cara's concerned tone compounded Rachel's fear. Then she thought—she wasn't home right now, and she had modern technology at her disposal. Thinking, for a brief moment like an *Englischer*, she dialed Mason's cell number from the reception phone. It rang out, no answer.

"Call again," Cara urged her, then, at another no answer, she shrugged. "He'll show up," she said and headed through to the back.

But Rachel wasn't so sure. She dialed another four times, gnawing the ends of her fingernails all the while—a bad habit she thought she'd broken long ago. She even left a voicemail. Two voicemails. Three.

Gott, please let him be okay, she prayed. It was a prayer that went unanswered. At nine-thirty, at Cara's insistence, they checked the local news.

Rachel's world stopped. There it was—a traffic collision involving an overturned truck and three cars. Seven dead. In the photograph under the headline was Mason's Toyota, his number plate just visible. Cara let out a shriek; Rachel dug her ragged nails into the palms of her hands in shock. Cara called the local hospital and got only vague answers. It was the police who told them that Mason's family had been notified and that Mason was dead.

Rachel's vision blurred and she couldn't breathe. Something was pressing on her chest. She grabbed her throat and pressed. She couldn't get air.

"Are you all right?" Cara cried, her voice rising. "Rachel! Rachel! Are you all right?"

No. No. No. She wasn't all right. She couldn't breathe. She was going to die right there. She slumped onto the desk, forcing herself to suck in air.

"Rachel!" Cara started to hit her back. "Rachel!"

Rachel prayed that she might die, too. Again, her prayer went unanswered.

Chapter Five

Rachel could barely remember her journey home that morning. Cara had decided they should close up the practice and cancel all appointments. Rachel went through the business of calling clients in a daze. She remembered walking out the door into the bright spring sunshine and thinking, *It should be raining. Why is the sun out? It should be raining.*

There was a storm brewing inside her, and it wasn't right that outside of her everything should be so clear and beautiful. How could someone die on such a glorious day?

She left the bicycle in the road, dismounting and then forgetting about it entirely. Mason... Mason *was dead*. How was that possible? It wasn't. The only conclusion Rachel could reach was that this was all some terrible dream. She had imagined it all. He would show up any minute.

She didn't make it to the front door of her house. Instead, she sat down at the edge of the road, her dress in the dirt. She stared down at the ground. Her eyes stung as hot tears flooded from them, running down her cheeks. Why was she crying? Mason wasn't dead. It was just a bad dream. It had to be...

"Rachel?" William's voice was both curious and worried.

Rachel stared at his feet, at the scuffs on his black shoes, the scraps of sawdust clinging to them. She couldn't speak, couldn't answer him.

"Rachel?" William said again, sounding scared now. Then, "I'll get *Mamm*."

Yes, *Mamm*. Rachel wanted her now—needed her. Needed to be sung to, needed her mother's arms around her. No... What she needed was her mother's practical, no-nonsense tone. Nothing's wrong. Get up off the floor and make yourself useful.

Mason was going to return any minute.

But there was nothing sharp in her mother's voice when she spoke. Rachel looked up at her, a fresh pang of pain at the worried look in her mother's eyes.

"Rachel? What on earth's the matter?"

Rachel cried out, then, and somewhere in that howl were the words, *He's dead. Mason's dead.* "I'm never going to see him again," she sobbed. And yet, still, she didn't quite believe her words.

Her mother helped her up, led her into the house and to her bed, where she got under the covers and lay very, very still. The tears stopped falling, and after a while, she fell asleep.

Rachel awoke to a knock on the door. For a moment, she couldn't remember a thing. And then it all came crashing down around her. Mason *was gone*.

Her mother entered the room with a bowl of hot soup. Rachel couldn't remember the last time she'd been excused from eating at the table. Perhaps once or twice, when she was ill as a child. But never in her adult life, certainly.

Rachel shook her head. She wasn't hungry. She couldn't possibly eat. Her stomach was leaden. Her heart was frozen.

"Nonsense. You have to eat," her mother scolded, and Rachel, knowing that tone, took the soup and tried. She swallowed several spoonfuls under her mother's watchful gaze, wishing she would go away, wishing she could just be alone...

"Tell me what happened," her mother said after a moment, but Rachel couldn't. If she talked about it, then it would be real. She didn't want it to be real.

Eventually, her mother left, the door clicking shut behind her.

Rachel left the bowl of soup unfinished on her bedside table.

It was evening when another knock on the door signaled the presence of her father. He, too, wanted to know what had happened. He wasn't as cautious as her mother, demanding an answer. So Rachel told him.

"Cars," he said, shaking his head. "Ridiculous things. Death traps. I've always said so."

Rachel swallowed her anger and turned away from him. When she didn't speak, he, too, eventually left her alone.

Rachel dozed on and off throughout the night, her dreams full of cars sliding off the road.

The next day, Rachel barely left her room at all. She couldn't face her family, couldn't face the world. It was now a world without Mason in it. If she stayed there, safe in her room where nothing bad could enter, she could pretend it wasn't true, that everything was just as it had always been.

Her mother brought her a breakfast of oatmeal, but this time Rachel left it untouched. She felt nauseous. If she ate anything, she would throw up for sure.

Around noon, her mother knocked on the door again. It would be more food, and Rachel pretended to be asleep.

Her mother came in anyway. "I know you're awake," she said.

Rachel groaned, as if she'd only just woken.

"You have a visitor," she said, her tone stern. "So you'd best get up and get dressed. You can hardly meet him in your nightgown."

Rachel's heart leapt. A visitor. And mother had said *he*. It was Mason, here to tell her it had all been some terrible mistake. He wasn't dead, and he felt just awful for the misunderstanding.

Hope roared through Rachel and she leapt from the bed, tearing off her nightgown and putting on her cape dress.

But it wasn't Mason waiting for her.

It was Lloyd, his expression sorrowful; although, when he saw Rachel, he forced a smile. Rachel didn't smile back. She couldn't. The muscles on her face just wouldn't work.

"I had to come," Lloyd explained. "When your mother told me, I-I knew you'd be feeling awful." He looked at her with such compassion. "That's a horrible understatement, I know."

"Thank you for coming," Rachel said, her words hollow, mechanical.

Lloyd had come to see her... it was unusual, to say the least. She could only assume that her mother or father had asked him to come. They were worried about her, she knew. What they thought Lloyd could do, she had no idea.

"I-I brought you something," Lloyd said, and held out a small, rectangular parcel, wrapped in cloth.

Rachel took it with only a dull sense of curiosity. It was a book, she realized, as she began to peel back the cloth. A book of poetry. *Wordsworth*. It was an old copy—the publishing date reading 1929.

"It may seem a little odd, but... this book was a great comfort to me," Lloyd told her. "It reminded me of the beauty in the world at a time when I struggled to see it. Besides the Bible, it was all I read for months at one point."

Rachel turned the book over in her hands. She had read a little of Wordsworth, once. *I wander lonely as a cloud*. What did that *mean*? How could clouds be lonely when they were always surrounded by other clouds?

"Thank you," she said, remembering her manners. She sat down opposite him. She read for a while, barely taking in the words. But staring at the pages gave her an excuse not to talk.

Lloyd didn't speak either. He picked up the worn Bible lying on the coffee table in front of him. He began idly leafing it through it, seemingly content to simply sit with her.

They remained like that for at least an hour, both of them only looking up when Rachel's mother entered the room with tea—or more likely, to check up on them.

Rachel couldn't deny Lloyd's presence was a comfort—he was quiet and didn't try to talk with her. He didn't ask questions or demand anything of her. He was just there. Rachel loved him a little for that.

Lloyd left the Raber house with a deep ache in his chest. He was used to that ache. It was always there around Rachel, but never this deep. Now, he felt her pain as if it were his own. He felt it and was unable to do anything about it.

He hoped the book he'd given her would be something of a comfort, and that she would realize what it really meant—that he was here for her, should she need anything.

There was little else he could for her now, he knew. So, he went back to work. Martha and Abraham were there, both of them working in the orchard, planting trees and watering the saplings. There was a wide variety of trees—apples, pears, and cherry trees. He'd started the orchard the previous year, after father had died. He'd needed a project then, something fresh and new to work on, that didn't remind him of *Dat*.

Now, those trees were growing strong. Just like the young boy that ran around the field, laughing and blowing whistles through blades of grass. Martha and Abraham's boy Isaac looked a lot like Martha had when she'd been a girl. Only he seemed to have inherited the family nose though. *Poor boy*, Lloyd thought, and smiled to himself.

Isaac ran to him now and wrapped his arms around Lloyd's leg. Lloyd lifted him up and whirled him through the air.

"And why aren't you helping your *mamm* and *dat*?" he asked.

"I helping," Isaac said, throwing both his arms out to either side.

Lloyd chuckled and set him down.

Once, he'd had that much energy too. He wished, for a moment, he could be that child again, have that much joy at such simple things. To run under the sun, no responsibilities.

But it was useless wishing, so instead, he set to work.

Chapter Six

Dear Diary,

If I thought I was lost before, I was wrong! I have never, ever, felt as lost as I am now. Mason is dead... Just writing those words seems wrong, somehow, like they're a lie. How can he be dead? He's so young! Was so young. Yes, older than me, I know, by almost ten years, but 31 isn't old. I just can't wrap my head around it. It doesn't make sense!

I don't know what I think writing this will achieve... Perhaps just to make some kind of sense of what I'm feeling right now, of what has happened. As if that's even possible!

I loved Mason. I know I kept my distance, but what else could I do? Now I almost wish that I hadn't, that I had loved him with everything I had. If only I'd known he would be taken from me, from the world, so soon.

But there was no way of knowing that. Only Gott *could have seen it coming, and it's not my place to wonder why he didn't stop it. I'm sure there were reasons, although I can't for the life of me imagine what they might have been.*

Yours,

Rachel.

The practice closed indefinitely, and of course, Rachel was out of her job. She had work to do—housework, office work for her father's business, and work around the farm. But she felt as if she'd lost her entire life in one fell swoop.

She went through it all with no heart and little mind. All she could think about was Mason, how maybe it was all a mistake —that he wasn't dead. She kept thinking she would see him again the following week, like he'd only gone on holiday. Of course, she knew she was being absurd, ridiculous, but she couldn't help it.

Everyone was being nice to her—no demanding requests, no teasing, not even from Adam, not even when she made some silly mistake that resulted in a mix-up with the furniture business.

Rachel sat through preaching service on Sunday, barely listening. She glanced at the other women around her, many of them still young. She wondered if any of them had secrets like hers—if any of them had lost someone close to them and been unable to tell anyone just how deeply it had affected them. She sang the slow songs, taking some small comfort in them.

Gott, she prayed. *Please help me deal with this loss. And not just me —care for Mason's family, his friends. We're all hurting now.*

She held her head up, her chin at a right angle, her back straight. Anyone who didn't know her well would never know that a piece of her had been crushed forever, ripped away from her.

The bishop spoke to her personally afterward, giving her his condolences and telling her to look to God for comfort. She would, of course—because where else could she look? This loss was beyond her understanding.

She didn't notice Lloyd Werngard talking with her brothers after the service, nor did she see him approaching across the path, her brothers' eyes on them both. She was glad for his presence, but when he spoke, she found she didn't want to hear his voice, to hear any more words of sympathy.

"Rachel," he said, but she didn't want to hear it, couldn't bear another inquiry about how she was doing. Part her still didn't want to believe Mason was dead—*What loss?* she kept thinking.

But instead Lloyd fell quiet, and after a moment, Rachel risked a glance at him. His face was calm, something steady about it that hadn't been there in their youth. When he spoke, his voice was calm, too. "Did you like the book?"

Rachel hadn't been expecting that. She'd read a few of the poems over the last few days, and knew one or two by heart now, even.

"I do. Thank you," she said, and she found she meant it. "I can see why the poems comforted you."

"I hope they can comfort you, too."

Rachel nodded. They had already, just a little. She'd spent most of her free time flipping through that book during the day, and the family Bible in the evening. She'd found some small comfort in each of them. Perhaps also because reading brought her some solitude, some peace, and some escape.

Lloyd opened his mouth, and then closed it again. He bounced on the balls of his feet for just a second. Funny—she hadn't noticed it before, but Lloyd was rarely ever still. He gestured freely when he talked, and he had a kind of nervous energy that could either be seen as endearing or annoying, depending on the mood.

Today, Rachel's mood was fraught. "What is it, Lloyd?" she asked. She'd meant her tone to be gently teasing, but instead her words came out as just plain rude.

Lloyd stilled and looked at her, his gaze unwavering. "I just wanted to thank you," he said, "for being there, you and your family, when my father passed. I was a little rude then, I fear.

I didn't want help. But I wanted to thank you for the offer of it. And if there's anything I can ever do for you now..."

Rachel forced a smile. "There's no thanks needed. It's just what neighbors do for one another."

"*Jah*," Lloyd agreed. "You're quite right. Still, my offer to you stands..."

When he got no reply, he simply nodded, turned, and walked away.

Rachel almost wished he hadn't left.

Lloyd felt weighted as he drove his buggy away after church, a small ache in his back that had been growing for days now causing him to wince. He pushed his shoulders back, straightening his stance as he rode the few miles back to his farm.

His parents' farm. His now, but always in the back of his mind he thought of it as theirs. They'd been the first Amish to farm it. Before that, it had belonged to *Englischers*. Their small community had been even smaller then. There had been no Lloyd, no Martha, no Emma. No Rachel, either, nor any of her brothers.

Rachel. He knew what she was feeling now. He'd never lost a friend, but he'd lost both his parents—his mother when he was a boy, and more recently, his father. It wasn't his business to speculate, but he was almost certain that Rachel had felt more strongly for Mason Porter than just a friend. She'd been in love with him, he was sure.

The look in her eyes when she'd talked about Mason was just how he imagined he looked—how he felt—when he thought about Rachel. He'd been angry when he'd first seen that. No, not angry. *Jealous*. And that, he knew, was wrong. It wasn't his place to judge her, not when his own feelings—that jealous anger that had come up in him—could also be judged. There was no human alive without sin. He could only try to be a better person. For himself, for Rachel, for God.

He wished he could take away Rachel's pain, the sadness and confusion that rested in her eyes now. But he couldn't. No one had been able to help him after his mother's death, nor his father's. No one except God, that was. It would be the same for Rachel. Only time and God's grace would heal her. Still, he had offered her what he could—he could be someone to talk to, someone who would listen, and perhaps understand.

He hoped she would, at some point, accept his offer, hoped she would come to him and release her burdens. Was there pride in that thought? he wondered. *Why do I need to be that person for her?*

The answer was simple: *I love her. I always have.* He wanted to be the one she could come to, to tell everything to. He also wanted to be strong enough to step back if she couldn't.

He'd loved Rachel since he was a little boy. He'd been unable then to leave her alone for too long, always trying to insert himself into her and Martha's games. His mother had told him often enough then to leave them alone, as had Martha, but Rachel hadn't seemed to mind...

A cool breeze struck his neck, and he quickened his pace. Summer hadn't yet arrived, and there was much still to be done at the farm.

Chapter Seven

The following week brought no return of Rachel's normality. She went once more back to the veterinary office—one afternoon to complete some paperwork and tidy up. The practice was quiet and empty, and every moment she expected to see Mason, with his kind smile and dark, curling hair. But she didn't.

Cara told her that Mason's brother had called a few days before to say the funeral would be the following Wednesday. They had delayed it so that family members who lived far away could attend.

A funeral... Yes, because Mason was dead. Rachel felt like a ghost herself, drifting along, outside of God's care. She prayed nightly to see Mason again somehow, for this to all be a terrible dream. It wasn't her place to question God's purpose, but still she couldn't help but wonder why.

She spent a few hours at the practice. It wasn't the same place anymore, not without Mason there, without the smell of coffee brewing in the little staff area, without the sound of him humming to himself as he moved from task to task.

Wednesday morning, Rachel's family gathered in the kitchen. Rachel wouldn't eat breakfast—couldn't—but she sat with her family nonetheless, bowed her head for silent prayer, and then pushed food around her plate.

Eventually they all piled into the buggy and *Dat* chivvied the horses into moving and they were off, on their way into Baker's Corner. None of them would have approved of Mason for her, not one, and yet here they were beside her. Rachel felt she should be grateful, but really all she wanted was to be alone.

Around the bend they met another buggy—Lloyd's. Martha and Abraham were riding in it, too, and a few miles down the road, she saw Joanne and John's smaller cart come out behind them.

Of course, many families around here knew Mason—he'd given advice and care to the community for years, helping the farmers to provide care to their animals. Many had known him, by sight at least. Naturally, they would want to pay their respects. Mason might have been an *Englischer*, but he was part of the community in his own way. An outsider, yes, but still connected.

The funeral was large, partly due to the Amish community's presence and partly due to the fact that Mason had come from a large family and had a lot of friends. Rachel wasn't sure where to sit, so she sat with her family. They were lucky to get seats at all—many were left standing at the back and at the far ends of the protestant church's aisles.

Rachel had never been to an *Englisch* funeral before but found similarities there. Differences, too—mainly to be in a church building, with stained glass windows and many other luxuries that Rachel found strange.

Mason had believed firmly in God, so it was a Christian funeral, with prayers and hymns. Rachel found herself barely able to sing them, however. She didn't know the words, and her voice wanted to crack at almost every syllable. She sat rigidly, straight-backed, her hands clasped firmly in her lap. She wanted to scream, to sob, to wail, but she couldn't. She would show nothing, reveal nothing to anyone.

After the funeral, many of her district peeled off from the slightly larger group of *Englischers*, but Rachel stayed, speaking with a few people she knew, offering condolences. It was easier, somehow, to give sympathy than to receive it.

As she turned to retreat back to the relative safety of her family, she almost bumped into Lloyd. He turned and offered her a slight, sad smile.

"I've never been to an *Englisch* funeral before," he said.

"I doubt anyone here has been to an Amish funeral, either," Rachel said idly.

"Strange, isn't it, how tragedy can sometimes bring two disparate communities together? Even if it's just for a short time."

Rachel nodded.

"Forgive me, because I know it's all anyone will be saying to you right now, but I truly am sorry. I know he was a good friend to you."

"He was a good man," Rachel said. "He'll be missed."

"I'm sure he will," Lloyd said. "There will be a hole, I imagine, in many lives now. Yours, too."

Rachel said nothing; she couldn't speak. If only Lloyd knew the size of it, a crater so deep there was almost nothing of her left. But if he knew, he wouldn't be standing here speaking to her. He would be ashamed of her, as she might have been of herself if—

But there was no if. There would never be an if. Whatever might have been between her and Mason was just imagination, speculative history.

"Keep busy," Lloyd told her, before moving off to speak with the bishop. "It helps."

Rachel was left alone, then, in a sea of people she didn't know and would, now, never know. She retreated to her mother's side, feeling like a small, nervous child.

She found, afterwards, that she could barely remember anything about the funeral. Not who was there, what was said, or even the order of events. Time seemed to shimmer and melt into itself. She could only remember that hollow, empty feeling, the incessant, hammering thought: *He's gone. Mason is really gone.*

He was gone, and yet everyone else who loved her was there, quietly supportive. They might not be aware of how deep her feelings for Mason really ran, but they all knew she'd lost someone—a boss and a friend.

In the days that followed, all she could do was follow Lloyd's advice—to keep busy. She threw herself into household chores, farm work, organizing files and records for her father's business. From sun-up to sun-down, she barely stopped for a moment. If she stopped, if she gave herself a moment to think, the overwhelming helplessness would take her over.

Lloyd visited often, sometimes with one of his sisters, Martha or Emma, sometimes without. He had business with her father, he said, and was discussing the sale of a small parcel of land with him, for reasons that Rachel had missed. He offered quiet words, which might have been comforting if Rachel had really listened to them.

William and Adam were less kind—they treated Rachel much the same as always. William was bossy, often patronizing, where Adam was teasing. Rachel preferred that. They didn't tiptoe around her. To them, very little had changed. They didn't see that inside Rachel, everything had changed.

One morning *Mamm* woke her early, before the sun had risen, ushering her out to do her morning chores. Rachel, now used to being the first one awake, found herself in a daze of confusion for the first half hour or so of the day, and muddled the order of things, feeding the goats before the chickens and forgetting entirely to check for eggs. Only when she was done did *Mamm* let her in on what was happening.

They were going to the Werngard farm that morning with Job and Catherine, to see the puppies Lloyd had told them about over dinner. That dinner had only been a few weeks ago, but it felt like a lifetime. Rachel had forgotten all about those puppies and all about Lloyd's offer to see them. She was surprised they were going at all. They hardly needed a dog along with their six goats and milking cow and horses. Rachel thought that perhaps her mother was trying to lift her spirits, to take her mind off of things.

Lloyd greeted them at the gate, wearing thick gardening gloves. He pulled them off and stuffed them in a pocket, the fingertips hanging loose. There was a little dirt smudge on the end of his long nose, and Rachel wanted almost to giggle. What a strange feeling! Laughter... When was the last time she had laughed? It felt like such a long time...

Lloyd's gaze lingered on Rachel for just a moment. She thought there was something in that look, almost a yearning, but then it was gone, and she put it out of her mind.

William had stayed behind with *Dat* to finish up some work with an *Englisch* customer, but Adam had taken a few hours off to come with them. Like Rachel, he had always been pretty keen on animals, and would hardly give up the chance to see baby ones. Rachel could see the excitement on his face, in the slight upturn of his lips and the way he almost bounced as he walked up the driveway. Rachel wanted to be excited too, but there was little joy left in her, it seemed.

She fell in behind *Mamm* and Catherine, who were chatting all things baby. A sliver of hope fluttered in Rachel's chest. The first of a new generation. She was going to be an *aenti*. She wished she could share that news with Mason. He was always talking about his nieces and nephews...

The hope she had felt evaporated. She would never hear those children's names again, never see the proud joy in his eyes as he talked about their latest exploits. She would miss that, too.

Lloyd led them out to the barn, where Bess greeted them with a wagging tail and a slow bump of her nose against Rachel's knees. Rachel bent to stroke her, out of sheer habit.

"Hello, girl." Bess licked her outstretched hand.

"She's a sweet thing," Job said, approvingly. "Who's the father?"

"One of the Danbers' dogs, a Shetland sheepdog, but I don't think any of these have inherited their father's coat. They all seem short to me."

"Short legs, too," Adam said, picking up a liver-spotted pup and holding him up to the light. The pup yapped and wagged his tail.

"How old are they, exactly?" Catherine asked, moving past Bess to look at the puppies herself.

"Eight weeks, so you could take one today if you wanted, although I'd rather keep them all for just a couple more weeks. It helps with their socialization, I feel."

Rachel hung back to let the others fawn over the puppies, keeping Bess company, who observed the process with a watchful eye. Rachel wondered what she thought of these strangers, coming in and handling her babies, potentially taking them away from her. At least, she supposed, Job and Catherine only lived a few miles down the road. Bess would see whichever pup they chose again, Rachel was sure of it.

"This one," Catherine decided, holding up a puppy that was more liver than white. She tried to lick her own nose, and Catherine smiled fondly.

Job nodded his assent. "She seems like a strong one," he said. "Hopefully, she'll turn out a hard worker."

"With the right training, they all will," Lloyd said confidently.

Rachel wondered how he knew, how he could sound so certain. Nothing in life was certain, she felt, except perhaps God.

Something nudged at her ankle, and Rachel looked down to see a small black and white puppy rolling in the straw at her feet. He rolled into her ankle again, and then a third time before righting himself. He had a black patch over one eye, shaped like a heart. Rachel watched him for a moment, and then bent to greet him with an outstretched hand. He licked her fingers, his tongue soft and warm. She smiled.

When she looked up, she saw her mother watching her, and then Lloyd, standing in the doorway, his gaze on her and the puppy.

"Does this one have a name?" she asked.

"Not yet. Except 'Runt'. Which isn't really a very nice name, I'm afraid."

"Oh." She looked back down at the puppy, who was sitting and wagging his little tail, brushing straw from side to side. "You should have a name."

"Maybe you can think of one," Lloyd said.

THE VET'S ASSISTANT

"His new owners will only go and change it again anyway, I suppose," Rachel said.

"I was thinking of keeping two of the pups, actually," Lloyd said. "I've only decided on one so far. Maybe you could choose the second."

Rachel smiled again. Trust Lloyd to be so considerate. "Then I would choose this one," she decided, and picked the pup up, cradling him in her arms.

Lloyd couldn't help but think of children when he saw Rachel cradling the smallest of Bess' pups. He'd never really considered whether he might want his own children or not before—it was pretty much a given that, if married, he would have them. But he'd never been especially fond of babies or small children in general. He supposed the thought was only in his mind because of Catherine's presence.

Either way, Rachel would make a good aunt, that was for sure. She was kind, considerate, and practical. She would be an asset in any child's life.

He shook these thoughts from his head, deciding it was improper, and besides, none of his business whether Rachel would be a good aunt—or mother. Yes, he felt as though there was something between them, but Rachel had given him no indication that she felt anything special, and they weren't courting, however much Lloyd might want to ask her.

He wouldn't ask now, he knew. Rachel had lost someone she loved. And yes, he was certain now that she had loved Mason Porter. Oh, he supposed nothing much had actually occurred between them—Rachel wasn't that sort of woman—but she'd loved him well enough. Which meant her loss was ten-fold.

That the puppies had coaxed a smile out of her, albeit a small one, was enough to make his day brighter. He missed that smile of hers, and seeing it now made his heart constrict. He hoped she'd smile again one day—really smile, the kind of smile she would feel in her heart, that would shine through her eyes.

That would take time, he supposed. Time. The great healer. She needed it more than anything now. And that was what he would give her. Time to heal. Then, perhaps, he could see where things stood between them.

They had lunch after that, Lloyd offering up a potato salad, green veggies, and delicious home-baked bread. Rachel hadn't known he could cook, although she supposed a man living alone had to learn at some point or another. She felt a pang of sympathy for him, then. She was so lucky, to still have both her parents and all her family around her. Lloyd still had his sisters, but he was an orphan. He'd lost his mother young, and she knew he'd been close to his father. It must have been hard, losing them. Rachel didn't know what she would do without her mother or her father.

Rachel helped *Mamm* clear the plates after dinner, taking them into the small kitchen to be washed and dried. They did their best at putting them away, and only a small handful of utensils were left sitting for Lloyd to take care of by the time they were done.

The house smelled the same as it had always smelled, faintly basil-y due to the herb garden outside the kitchen window. Rachel breathed in that smell, so familiar. It was comforting. She knew Lloyd's home so well, as if it were almost her own home. She had played here so often when she was young and had attended church here in the years since.

It was a comfort, to be in a house that was familiar and yet not her own, not fraught with her own sadness. She had spent too long inside, she supposed. Yes, she worked in the office next to her father's workshop a few hours a day and did her chores around the farm. She fed the goats and the chickens, collected eggs, helped with weeding and pruning and fencing.

Inside, she wasn't kept idle either—she sewed and mended clothes, did the washing, the ironing, the cleaning, and when she had time to spare, she knitted warm clothes for Catherine and Job's unborn baby. Still, none of that was the same as going out into the world, being somewhere *else*. A change of scenery—yes, it was just what she needed.

And the puppies were very sweet. She almost wished she could take one home with them, but even if *Mamm* and Adam were on her side about that, she knew *Dat* wouldn't be.

She found herself, for the first time in a while, almost enjoying herself. She realized, later, she had barely thought about Mason while she there at all.

Chapter Eight

The furniture the Raber's made was truly wonderful to look at. Daniel Raber had a God-given gift, a way of working that ensured everything he made was robust as well as beautiful. There was nothing fanciful about his designs—everything was made with purpose in mind, but it was beautiful nonetheless. He knew exactly the right sort of woods to choose, the best way to let the natural beauty shine through, how to showcase knots and color in perfect position.

Lloyd couldn't help but turn his head this way and that as William led him through the workshop to where Daniel was busy hammering nails into a piece of wood that looked like nothing much yet, but, Lloyd supposed, soon would.

"The land is yours," Lloyd told him. "Ten acres of good

pasture. I can't keep up with it—it's far too steep for me with so little help. But if your sons want it, it's good for livestock."

Daniel paused in his wood and stood, brushing sawdust off himself. "Thank you, Lloyd. Do you have the paperwork?"

Lloyd nodded. He would hardly have come here after weeks of discussion without it. "It's all in order. All you have to do is sign."

They shook hands, then, and Daniel filled out his share of the paperwork. Lloyd would pass it on to his lawyer in the morning, but it was already evening now, too late to be bothering him.

"Would you stay for dinner?" Daniel asked, and Lloyd gladly accepted. Dinner at the Rabers' meant seeing Rachel again. It had been a few weeks since she and her family had come to see the puppies, and the one she'd picked out was just as big as any of the others now, no longer the runt.

Rachel was in the front room, reading, when he entered. She was the first person he saw—the rest of the house was quiet. He'd expected to see Ellen in the kitchen—Daniel had told him she'd be around—but there was no sign of her. So he found himself alone with Rachel. Although he'd run through a dozen or more scenarios that began like this one, he couldn't think of a single word to say. Eventually, he settled for, "Hello."

She set aside her book. "Lloyd," she said, and the sound of his name on her lips was beautiful. "How are you? How are the puppies?"

"They're *gut*," he told her. "Have you thought of a name for the little one you liked?"

She smiled at that. "I have," she said. "But you have to guess first."

Lloyd groaned. He hated guessing games. His sisters had made him play them all the time as children. Still, this was Rachel, so he decided to play along. "Patch?" he suggested.

Rachel shook her head, a secretive smile crossing her face.

"Sir Barks-a-lot?"

Rachel chuckled at that. "One more guess," she said. "Then I'll tell you."

"Wordsworth," he offered, knowing already that it wouldn't be right.

She waved the book she was reading at him. He barely caught the title—*Pride and Prejudice*.

"Darcy," she said.

Lloyd groaned. "Of course," he said. "I should be more observant, clearly." He considered it for a moment. It was a good sort of name. Certainly better than 'Sir Barks-a-lot'.

"Darcy it is," he decided.

"Have you read this book?" Rachel asked him, waving the book again.

"Once," Lloyd said. "It was my sister Emma's favourite. She loved it so much she didn't want me to borrow it. Unfortunately, I have little time for reading these days, but perhaps I'll make time for another read soon. I barely remember the plot, I'm afraid."

"Well," Rachel said. "If you barely remember it, you can relive it as though it's all new to you. I love doing that with books sometimes. You always see different sides to it, too. Especially if a few years have passed."

Lloyd agreed. "Yes, I suppose experience does change your view of things, at least a little."

Rachel nodded, but her gaze cast downwards, pensive. Lloyd supposed her recent experiences hadn't been very favorable. He wished he'd changed the subject.

Then she seemed to brighten, all at once. "Are you staying for dinner? *Mamm's* gone to gather herbs and eggs, but she'll be back soon."

"I am," Lloyd said, and his heart lightened. She seemed happy that he was going to be staying, and that, at least, gave him hope. "Where's your brother Adam today? I haven't seen him."

Rachel smirked, a mild thing, but new to Lloyd. "Oh, he's out courting Laura Farmer. Apparently, they've become quite close. Although, Adam thinks its still a secret."

Lloyd's eyebrows rose almost to his hairline. "Really? I never would have thought. They seem very different."

"Sometimes things work like that. I think she complements him rather nicely. Although I'm not sure *he* complements her the same."

Lloyd chuckled. "I'm sure he must," he said. "Otherwise it will never work."

"Well he certainly seems very upbeat about it all," Rachel said. "I never really imagined Adam courting anyone, but I think he might very well love her. At least in his way."

"And what of William? He still isn't courting anyone?"

"Not that any of us know of. Although he's been much quieter than usual lately, so perhaps there is someone on the horizon. Or not..." Rachel shook her head then. "I don't normally gossip this much, but, well... they are my brothers, so I suppose that's all right."

"I suppose it is," Lloyd said. He rarely gossiped himself, but he didn't mind listening to it occasionally. Especially when it was coming from Rachel, and even more so when she sounded so happy about it. Perhaps she was already beginning to heal from her loss.

But he couldn't assume that. No, it was still too early. He took a seat—although Rachel hadn't offered—and they sat for a while, discussing her brothers and then, when that topic ran out, books again. She seemed in less pain, certainly, but there was still a sort of melancholy in her eyes.

Lloyd returned home that evening feeling both joyous and sad. Dinner had been pleasant, and he marveled at how comfortable and at ease he felt with Rachel's family. He felt for Rachel, though, for her loss. He prayed for her recovery, that she would soon see the wonder in the world again, that she would heal and move on with her life. She was young, and he didn't doubt that she would, but there was no harm in a little divine help along the way.

He spent the later part of his evening doing his rounds of the farm, checking that the chicken coops were securely shut, that the sheep were all present and none had rolled over onto their backs. He returned to his kitchen for a cup of hot cocoa, then retreated to bed.

A week later, Lloyd was once again at the Raber house. This time, it wasn't on business or by invitation. He had, finally, come to a decision.

He found Daniel in his workshop, which was where he seemed to be most days. Adam and William were there too, and both greeted him warmly. Daniel emerged covered in sawdust, a chisel in his hand.

"Lloyd, what a pleasant surprise. What brings you here so early?"

Lloyd wondered at that—for it didn't seem very early to him. He'd been up well before sunrise, taking care of his animals, and then out in the orchard undertaking some much-needed pruning work.

"I'd like to talk to you," he said, his voice lowered, not wanting Rachel's brothers to hear him and start speculating, "about a private matter."

Daniel frowned, but gestured through to the back section of his workshop, away from interested ears.

"What's the matter?" Daniel asked, a concerned edge to his voice.

"Oh, it's nothing like that," Lloyd assured him. "I would like to ask you..." He faltered, his nerve ebbing. "Well..."

"Spit it out," Daniel said, a little roughly. He was a busy man —Lloyd supposed he had no time for dilly-dallying.

"I'd like to ask your advice about..."

"Courting my daughter?" Daniel was smiling now.

"Well, yes..."

Daniel chuckled, a deep, throaty sound. "Well, I'm not surprised at your interest. Not at all. It's a bit of a surprise to have you ask me about it. I figured you'd keep it secret if you ever decided to pursue her. But I s'pose, given the circumstances..."

Lloyd felt foolish. Why had he felt compelled to talk to Rachel's father about this?

"Ellen and I always hoped..." Daniel said. "But I suppose you'll have to ask Rachel, first, before you know for certain. My advice would be to approach her. But you do know that Rachel's not been entirely herself lately, I'm afraid."

Lloyd nodded. "I know. I plan to approach the matter rather carefully, give her some time to think about it."

Daniel nodded. "Very wise," he agreed. "Now, I'm afraid, Lloyd, that I've a lot of work to do. But we'll catch up later in the week."

Lloyd agreed. He would see the Rabers at preaching service that Sunday, if not before. Whether or not he would ask Rachel then, he wasn't sure. He would have to make a plan...

Chapter Nine

Diary,

I wonder whether I should keep this book or burn it on the fire. It's so full of secrets. Anyone who found it would surely be ashamed of me. But perhaps, too, they would feel some sympathy for me. Not that that's at all what I want. No, I want to live life as normal, to be part of the world again. Mason would want that for me, I'm sure.

I must make myself useful now and pray to Gott to give me a chance to do so.

With Mason, I felt as though I had some purpose—we were healing, helping animals and owners alike. Of course, Mason did most of that healing. I only answered the phones and organized the files. But that certainly had its uses. I don't think I will ever be part of the Englisch world again in that way. I don't think I would want to be. I only stayed, really, for the job and for Mason. Without either, there is no reason for me to be there. I was never really part of it anyway, simply on the fringes. I know Dat *and probably* Mamm *too, though she would never say as much, thought that I was being too influenced by that world, but I don't think now that that was ever true.*

I love my home, my district, my family. I don't think I would have ever left them, not even for Mason, although I'll admit—and as you already know—I was torn for a while.

I will always love Mason, I think. I will always miss him. I can't help that. But I am hopeful that one day, and perhaps even one day soon, my heart will heal just enough. Just enough so I can go on living, so I can be useful, and maybe, maybe, love again.

Yours,

Rachel.

Rachel finished church service that morning feeling refreshed. She hadn't felt so good in months, not since Mason... But she didn't want to think about that now. Not when she felt so connected to everything. Mason, she was sure, was with God. She would see him again some day, she supposed. She had to believe that.

Lloyd was to take her home that day, and she waited for him outside, a little apart from the groups of chatting young men and women. Rachel could have joined them, but she wanted to embrace the quiet, the sound of crickets singing and the wind through the treetops—the sounds of God.

She saw Lloyd from a distance and began to walk toward where he was chatting with a small group of young men. He turned, saw her, and peeled away from them.

They wandered over to the rows of buggies and he helped her up into his buggy, always the gentleman, and climbed up beside her. He was quiet for a while, and that suited Rachel. She listened instead to the sound of the horses' hooves clopping over the ground, to the wheels rolling, clunking over the occasional stone.

Eventually he said, "Rachel..."

She turned to him. He seemed nervous, his lips pressed into a thin line, his gaze focused on the road ahead.

"Yes?" she asked, when he said nothing more.

"I was wondering, perhaps... if you... if you..."

She bit her tongue on a laugh. "If I what?"

"If you'd, perhaps, like to go riding with me regular-like..."

She almost did laugh, then, for the pure joy of his question. He wanted to court her—that was certainly what he meant. A young man didn't ask a girl to ride with him regularly unless he wanted to court her.

His question meant that somehow, maybe, her world was

righting itself. She wasn't sure how she felt about. Not really. But still... She smiled at him.

"I'll think about it," she said, and that was a promise—she really would think about it.

She thought about it even as they drove home. Lloyd was funny, sweet, and had all the qualities she admired in others. He was a godly man, always attended church, and led by example. He worked hard. He was compassionate and considerate. And, yes, she liked him. Perhaps not in a deep, passionate way, but that wasn't everything. She could see herself living a good sort of life with Lloyd.

She went to bed that night still thinking about it, about Lloyd, about his kind face. And also, about Mason, about the past, and the future.

Surprisingly, she slept soundly.

Rachel gave Lloyd her answer almost a week later. She hadn't meant to make him wait so long, but it was a big decision, and the question of whether or not she and Lloyd would be suitable as husband as wife was difficult to answer. They'd known each other a long time, been friends almost as long.

To change that from friendship... It could ruin everything. But then again, it could open up new possibilities, and Lloyd had been so kind to her. He'd given her space, and more than that, he'd treated her as normal and hadn't tiptoed around her grief. He'd spoken to her with dignity and given her some kind of normality.

So, she told him yes.

His sun-tanned face lit up, breaking into a wide smile. "You won't regret it," he promised, and Rachel laughed. She hadn't for a moment thought that she would. It wasn't marriage yet, after all. They were simply testing the waters. She might feel regret if the friendship they had was ruined, but she wouldn't regret courting him, taking a chance with him. Besides, Lloyd was decent in every way. She couldn't imagine them ever not being friends.

They turned into the driveway of Rachel's family home, and Lloyd stopped the cart a few meters from the door.

"May I call on you tomorrow?" he asked.

Rachel considered it for a moment, thinking about everything she had to do tomorrow—she had promised her father she'd put in a few hours in the office, but she knew he wouldn't mind if she left a little early. He liked Lloyd. So she nodded, and the smile he gave her warmed her heart, just a little.

Chapter Ten

Dear Diary,

I miss Mason so much, even after months. I had never imagined I could feel this way, hurt so deeply... I know Gott is testing me; we must all go through hardships in life. Or perhaps he is punishing me... But no, I can't think like that. Before, I was soft, fanciful. Now I know what horrors life can bring, and that I can—and must—endure them. I know I am being made strong. And I am healing, I think, in a way. In the same way that torn flesh will heal into tougher scar tissue.

Lloyd asked me if I would like to be courted by him. He said it just like that, so formally! Today I said yes. I'm not sure, but can anyone ever be really sure about such a thing? I am fond of Lloyd, and I think, maybe, I'm starting to see more in him, that I'm starting to fall for him. But I can't be sure. I still don't think of it as LOVE, in all capitals. My heart is still a step behind me, in the past, with Mason.

But I feel that maybe, one day... At least, I hope so, for I can imagine sort of a good life with Lloyd, and I am fond of him.

I pray that Gott *continues to give me the strength to endure. I know the future must hold so much. If only I can catch up to the present. I must, now, live in the moment, and be fully present during whatever time I may have on this earth. I believe Mason wouldn't want anything less for me.*

Yours,

Rachel.

Rachel tucked her diary back under her mattress. She lay with her hands beneath her head, staring up at the ceiling, wondering what life might have in store for her. Lloyd... Could he really be the one? Life on his farm, with dogs and children... Yes, a simple sort of life. Peaceful. That was what she needed now. Peace.

She tossed and turned that night, unable to sleep, thinking of Lloyd, and of Mason, trying to fit the pieces together in her head. Eventually she gave up on sleep, and crept downstairs to make herself a cup of camomile tea.

She was startled by a creak of a floorboard and turned to see Adam standing there in his nightshirt, a sheepish look on his face.

"You were going to sneak up on me and scare me half to

death, weren't you?" Rachel said, already reaching for another mug for him.

Adam shrugged. "You can't sleep either?"

"*Nee*. But why can't you?"

"Too many thoughts," he said, as though that revealed anything. Rachel accepted the answer, though, and poured him out some tea. He took it, retreating to the small table they used for breakfasts and teatime.

They sat in companionable silence for a while, before Adam drained his mug, stretched, and announced that he was heading back to bed. Rachel stayed up for the better part of an hour, had a second cup of tea, and then followed suit.

This time, she found her eyes drifting shut almost immediately. *Lloyd*, she thought.

Lloyd couldn't sleep. He was both excited and nervous for the following afternoon, and kept tossing and turning, too hot, and then, with the covers thrown back, too cold. Eventually, he sat up, and reached for his Bible. Reading *Gott's* word would help put things in perspective, he hoped.

An hour later, he felt calmer, but he still wasn't quite ready to go back to sleep. He got up, and, still in his nightclothes, went outside, into the dark. Crickets sang in the night air, and there was a soft breeze rippling through the wheat to his right. He thought, then, that this too was God's word. His voice, his mind, in all things.

Lloyd tilted his head up to gaze at the stars. It was a moonless night, and the sky was crowded with stars. He wrapped his arms around himself, hoping that tomorrow would be all right. He wanted things to be perfect.

I love her, he thought to himself, not for the first time and almost certainly not for the last. She'd given him a chance, *the* chance, the one he'd been waiting so long for. He had to make this work, he knew. But what if...

What if she still wasn't ready, if she still wasn't over Mason Porter? There was no way he could compete with a dead man. There was no way he could have competed with him alive, either. His only chance there had been that cultural divide keeping Rachel and Mason apart. He knew that. He would be second best, he supposed, but oh well. What was the harm in that, really? He loved Rachel, and perhaps she could love him too, one day.

Chapter Eleven

Lloyd called for her just after noon the next day. Rachel had finished up her work early and was just leaving her father's workshop when she heard his cart pulling up outside the house. She walked toward him and smiled.

He produced a bunch of wildflowers from behind his back, and she blinked for a moment before taking them. "Thank you," she said, breathing in the floral scent.

"A small gesture," he said, waving it away as though it were nothing.

She motioned Lloyd to come inside with her. She placed the flowers in a small vase of water on the kitchen windowsill and gestured for Lloyd to take a seat.

"Would you like tea?" she asked, but he shook his head.

"Actually, we should get going," Lloyd said. "I have an errand to run first, you see."

"How romantic," Rachel teased.

Lloyd laughed.

She called good-bye to her mother, who was in the front room, likely crocheting a new blanket for the baby, and Lloyd mentioned that they would be back before dark.

Rachel grinned at him. "Come on," she said, and led the way out to his cart.

They took a winding, bumpy ride through the countryside. The errand, it turned out, was a brief stop at Lloyd's elder sister, Emma's, house. Rachel had only been here a few times for church, and knew that Noah, Emma's husband, had a small cheese-making business.

Lloyd darted into the house, leaving Rachel to wait in the cart.

When Lloyd returned, he was carrying a small bundle under one arm, and he placed it in the back of the cart.

"Are you done?" Rachel asked, in mock-annoyance.

"Almost," Lloyd said.

They stopped again a few houses down, at the Millers', who, contrary to their name, mostly made soap and jam.

Lloyd was inside only a few minutes before he emerged again, all apologies, and jumped back up onto the cart beside her.

"I hope this afternoon isn't just going to be a tour of all the local houses," Rachel said, eyebrows raised.

Lloyd chuckled. "Be patient," he told her.

They continued on until they reached the river. Lloyd followed it for half a mile and then stopped the cart. He got down, secured the reins, and then helped Rachel down as well.

From the back of the cart he pulled away a cloth, revealing an old wicker hamper. He heaved it out, and Rachel got the sense it was pretty heavy.

"A picnic?" She realized, excited now. She loved picnics.

"Well observed," he teased.

They picked a shady spot beneath a willow tree, its long tendrils trailing through the water. Lloyd opened the hamper, and Rachel peered inside.

"Lloyd!" she exclaimed. He'd definitely overdone it. There were several small pots in there, a jar of fine blueberry jam, bread, cheese, cold meats, and fruit.

He began to lay it all out, along with plates and cutlery. "Shall we offer thanks?" he suggested.

Rachel bowed her head, and silently spoke words of thanks.

Thank you, Gott, for all this wonderful food. For our community, who can work such wonders with what they have, for the land on which we can grow and work. She had planned to finish there, but instead, she prayed one more silent sentence. *Thank you for giving us strength to endure tragedy, and for the ability to begin things anew.*

She looked up and Lloyd who was also finished with his silent prayer. Together, they said, "Amen."

Lloyd opened one of the pots—a creamy potato salad with scallions and chives. Rachel took three heaped spoonfuls of it. She opened another to find a light salad, with lettuce, spinach, beetroot, tomatoes, and cucumber.

They ate with a cool breeze playing around them, filling themselves with God's bounty. Rachel leaned back after her plate was clear. "That was wonderful *gut*," she said. "Thank you, Lloyd."

But they weren't finished yet. Lloyd unwrapped the cheese he'd collected from his sister's house—pungent Brie and began layering it onto thick slices of bread.

"Oh, I couldn't," Rachel said, when Lloyd handed her a slice. But, she found, she could.

She had a few slices of apple for dessert, and then, truly, she was finished.

"This is lovely," she admitted, looking out across the water at the ducks swimming there, the sun shimmering on the surface. It was almost summer now—May beginning to blend into June.

They talked for a while, then, Rachel moving to a sunnier spot to feel the warmth on her face.

Rachel told him about her brothers' latest exploits, and Lloyd shared new details about the puppies, Darcy in particular.

"And the sheep," Lloyd said. "Five of them escaped on me again last night."

"The same ones?"

Lloyd shook his head. "The same leader. She picks a new group to lead astray every time."

Rachel laughed at that. "That's what you get for working with animals," she told him.

As the sun grew lower in the sky, they cleared up their things, mindful that Rachel had to be back before dark. They piled everything back into the cart and climbed in. Watching the sun begin to set, Lloyd urged the horses into a trot.

"Can we make a stop?" Rachel asked. He cast her a curious glance but nodded. Today had been wonderful, but Rachel still felt as though something wasn't quite right, as though there was something she needed to do.

She was quiet during the ride, and she knew that Lloyd noticed, because he kept glancing over at her. Still, she didn't feel quite like explaining right now.

She directed Lloyd to the cemetery adjacent to the church where Mason's funeral had been held. She felt, rather than saw, Lloyd's understanding.

"Would you like me to come with you?" he asked.

Rachel shook her head. This, she needed to do alone.

She climbed down from the cart, relieved that Lloyd respected her wishes, and didn't argue or try to follow her.

She plucked a few small flowers from the roadside—mostly daisies, with a few crocuses, and carried them with her through the cemetery gates.

She couldn't quite remember where Mason had been buried. Strange; she'd thought that would be something etched in her memory forever. She wound her way through the rows, glancing over names and dates. So many people, some even younger than Mason. And then, she came across Mason's name.

The grave was in a sunny, easterly spot, and buttercups grew up through the grass around it. His headstone was a simple one. The inscription below his name and the dates that bookended his life read *Beloved Son and Brother. Go in Peace.* Rachel knelt down beside it and ran her hands along that inscription. Mason would never be anything more than that— never a husband, never a father. He never would have been her husband, whether he'd lived or not; she realized that now. Still, Rachel knew she had been blessed to have known him.

He had touched so many lives, brought so much joy to the world. Brought joy to *her*.

But now, she felt, it was time to move on. She would always love Mason, in a way, and always mourn him. But there was, now, the promise of a bright future.

She glanced back toward the gates, where the cart, and Lloyd, waited beyond.

"I have to go now," she told Mason. "But I'll come back again. I promise."

She clasped her hands together, then, and prayed. She prayed for Mason, for healing, not just for herself, but for all Mason's friends and family. They, too, would always be in her thoughts, for she knew their pain.

She stood, brushing off her dress, and took a last glance at that inscription, at the mound of earth where the grass was only just beginning to grow again. *Gott keep you*, she thought, and walked away.

Lloyd dropped Rachel off that evening with a sombre expression. Rachel turned to him, not wanting to leave him quite yet. "Thank you," she said.

He blinked, surprised. "For what?"

"For today. For every day these past few months. You've been such a comfort, Lloyd. So understanding—"

Lloyd reached to her, then, and clasped her hands in his. His palms were work-rough and warm. He smiled, a soft, tender thing. "Thank *you*," he said.

"For what?" Rachel asked then laughed.

Lloyd's eyes crinkled with amusement. "For being you. For being in my life. For wanting to support me when father died. I didn't want help then, but... I'm glad I could at least be there for you when you needed it. Thank you for not pushing me away."

Rachel wriggled one of her hands free and brushed his cheek with her fingertips. Lloyd's face was smooth—he never seemed to grow any stubble at all.

"I might have tried," she whispered. "But you were so quiet, you didn't give me any reason to."

Lloyd chuckled. "Most of the time when people say I'm too quiet, they don't mean it as a compliment."

"Well, I do," Rachel said. "So many people just want to talk talk talk, to tell you how to go about things, all the things you should do to make yourself feel better. Honestly, I couldn't stand it, Lloyd."

"Neither could I. That's why I didn't."

"Rachel," *Dat's* voice called from the doorway of the house.

Rachel turned and waved to him, then turned back to Lloyd. "Thank you for today, too," she said. "I really enjoyed myself."

"*Gut*," he said, and then released the hand he was still holding. Rachel mourned the loss of that warmth, but it was time to go. Her parents were waiting. Likely, the evening meal would be going cold. She climbed down from the cart and started across to the house.

"I'll see you soon," Lloyd called to her, something in his voice making Rachel turn.

"*Jah*," Rachel said, smiling.

Yes, she thought so. Lloyd had given her hope, hope for a new start, a new life, a future.

She watched his cart go, and for the first time in a while, she was excited for the days to come.

Epilogue

Dearest Diary,

It's been a long time since I last wrote. Funny, but I found this book in with my things, although I'd thought I had thrown it out.

I married Lloyd last spring, after almost a year of courting. And yes, I'm sure you want to know whether I love him now. I can tell you I do. Love can come about in all sorts of ways, I think. With Lloyd, it took time, but when he asked me to marry him, I said yes right away. I didn't even need to think about it.

Things are changing again, very soon. I am surrounded by love. The love of Lloyd, of my family, my community, and of course Gott's love.

This will be my last entry, I'm afraid. Really, I am only filling you in for old time's sake, and because there are so few pages left. It seems wrong to leave them empty, somehow.

A small part of me does still love and miss Mason Porter, but it's somehow shrunk in size now, taking up less of me. I'm not sure how I feel about that. Guilty, in a way, as though perhaps it was not true love, as I had thought. But no, there is still something there. I think there will always be something. But I have room for so much more now. I am excited not just for my future, but for my present, too.

Yours,

Rachel.

Rachel sat on the porch, sipping iced tea. The sun was shining. Lloyd was beside her, his knee touching hers. She savoured that warmth, that connectivity. They'd been married almost a year, now, but she still enjoyed being close to Lloyd.

She looked out at the stretch of grass before them, where her nephew ran and her niece crawled. Her nieces and nephews by marriage were there, too, running around and playing with sticks. The air around them was full of their laughter.

It was a little crowded on the porch, the chatter of grown-ups not quite drowning out the shrieks of the children. *Mamm* and *Dat* sat opposite them, with William, Job, and Catherine. Adam and Laura were there too, married just a few months ago now. Lloyd's sisters, too, were there, with their husbands. Normally, neither Lloyd nor Rachel would enjoy such a gathering, but today was special. Rachel suppressed a broad grin, certain it would give her away.

Bess lay at Rachel's feet, chewing on a bone and ignoring the people around him, while Darcy and his sister, Lily, played with the children, who had started throwing the sticks for them.

Rachel laughed watching them all. Goodness, but she was happy!

Lloyd glanced at her. Was now the time? Nerves fluttered through her, and she set down her glass, wiped her palms on her apron. She cleared her throat. "We have something to share," she said.

Her mother gasped, already jumping to conclusions—albeit the right ones. "Don't tell me I'm going to be a *mammi* again!" she said, already grinning.

"Goodness, you had to guess, didn't you?" Rachel chastised.

Her mother had the good grace to look sheepish, at least.

"Didn't I tell you?" Catherine said to Job, nudging him in the ribs.

He smiled ruefully. "Thinks she knows everything, this one."

"I'm sure she does," *Mamm* said idly.

"I suppose now it's my turn to knit clothes for your little one," Catherine said, then.

Brimming with joy, Rachel excused herself after a few

moments, retreating into the quiet of the kitchen. It was almost too much—too much happiness, too much love.

Lloyd poked his head around the door. "Everything all right?" he asked.

Rachel nodded, smiling. "Everything's perfect," she said.

Lloyd crossed the kitchen toward her, opening his arms wide. She stepped into them, savoring his warmth, his earthy scent.

"Come on," he said. "Everyone's waiting to congratulate you some more. Or I could tell them you've come down with morning sickness and gone to bed?"

Rachel chuckled. Lloyd was always so thoughtful. "I couldn't do that to them," she told him.

"I suppose not," he said. Then he took in a deep breath. "Well then. Come on." He stepped back and offered her his hand instead. She took it, and they walked back out onto the sunny porch together.

The End

Thank you for Reading

If you **love Amish Romance**, <u>**Visit Here:**</u>

http://ticahousepublishing.subscribemenow.com

to find out about all **New Hannah Miller Amish Romance Releases! We will let you know as soon as they become available!**

If you enjoyed ***The Vet's Assistant!*** would you kindly take a couple minutes to leave a positive review on Amazon? It only takes a moment, and positive reviews truly make a difference. I would be so grateful! Thank you!

Turn the page to discover more Hannah Miller Amish Romances just for you!

More Amish Romance from Hannah Miller

Visit HERE for ALL of

Hannah Miller's Amish Romances:

http://www.ticahousepublishing.com/amish-miller.html

About the Author

Hannah Miller has been writing Amish Romance for the past seven years. Long intrigued by the Amish way of life, Hannah has traveled the United States, visiting different Amish communities. She treasures her Amish friends and enjoys visiting with them. Hannah makes her home in Indiana, along with her husband, Robert. Together, they have three children and seven grandchildren. Hannah loves to ride bikes in the sunshine. And if it's warm enough for a picnic, you'll find her under the nearest tree!

Manufactured by Amazon.ca
Bolton, ON